"Rise and shine, Solomon,"
Mr. Johnson says to his son,
"Today we are going to India!"

1

With his dad's help, Solomon quickly packs his bags and together they are off on their great adventure.

When Mr. Johnson and Solomon land in India, Solomon waves to the other children, but they press their palms together with a slight bow and a smile. This is how they greet in India.

3

After seeing how the children are dressed, Solomon realizes that he needs new clothes.

He goes to the clothing store and says "Hello" to the store clerk. The clerk smiles at Solomon and replies "Namaste," which is used as both a greeting and for saying farewell in the Hindi language.

4

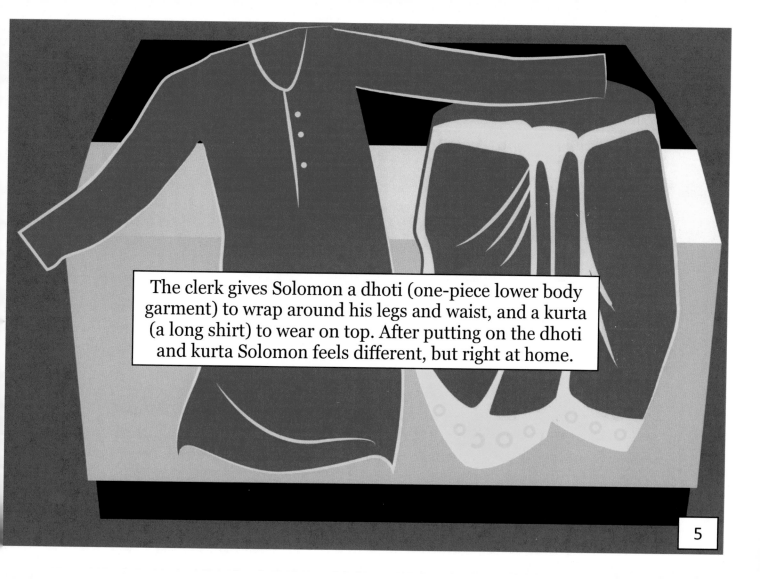

The clerk gives Solomon a dhoti (one-piece lower body garment) to wrap around his legs and waist, and a kurta (a long shirt) to wear on top. After putting on the dhoti and kurta Solomon feels different, but right at home.

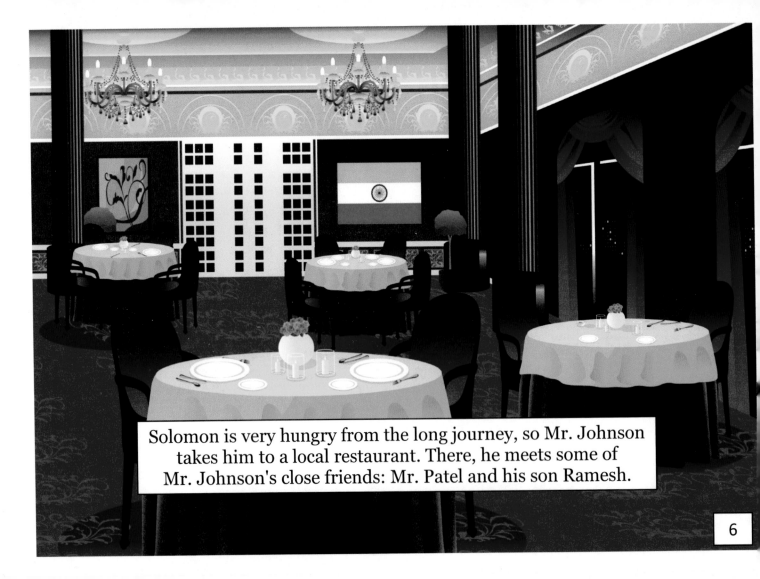

Solomon is very hungry from the long journey, so Mr. Johnson takes him to a local restaurant. There, he meets some of Mr. Johnson's close friends: Mr. Patel and his son Ramesh.

The group of four sit at a table and eat delicious roti (a flat bread), steamed rice and spicy vegetable curry.

After eating, Mr. Johnson has to go take care of some business, so Solomon's Indian friends take him to the market. There they drink chai (a tea mixed with milk) which they purchase from a street vendor.

All around them are crowds of people going in and out of stalls and small shops, which are selling so many different interesting things.

Solomon wants to find out what Indian children like to play, so Ramesh takes him to the park. There a group of kids who are playing field hockey invite Ramesh and Solomon to join.

After a long, hot, tiring game, Ramesh and Solomon go back inside where Mr. Patel has 2 large glasses of mango lassi (a cold smoothie made of milk, yogurt and sugar) waiting for them.

12

It is time for the children to learn something new. Mr. Patel teaches Solomon and Ramesh how to design textiles, since that is his profession.

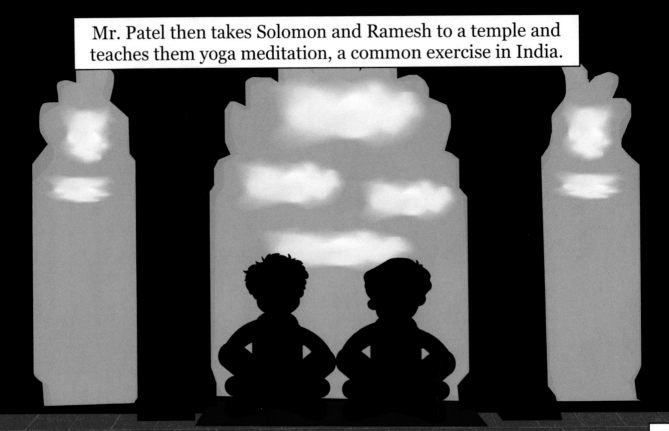

It starts to get late, and it is time for Solomon to get some rest, so Mr. Johnson picks him up from the temple and they go to sleep at a nearby hotel.

They wake up early the next morning to the sound of birds singing and chirping. Solomon goes to look outside and is amazed to see such birds of beautiful color.

As soon as Solomon gets dressed in his kurta, he is happily greeted by some more visitors to the country.

"Surprise!" says Mrs. Johnson, as she enters into the hotel room with Solomon's little sister, Mary.

Now that the entire family is together in India, Mr. Johnson decides that he should take time off from work and spend the day sightseeing with them.

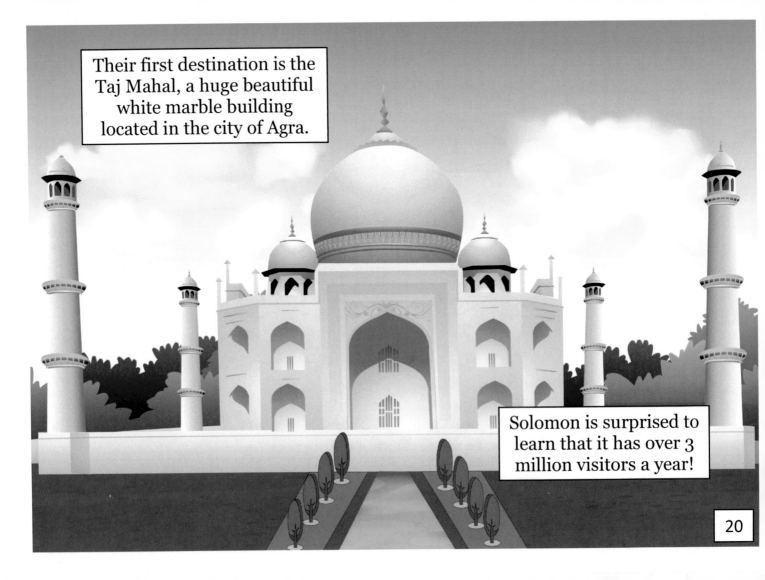

Their first destination is the Taj Mahal, a huge beautiful white marble building located in the city of Agra.

Solomon is surprised to learn that it has over 3 million visitors a year!

20

Next the Johnson family goes to visit Hampi, a laid back village which was developed over 1500 years ago! Mary is very impressed with the good condition of over 500 monuments found in these ancient ruins.

Mrs. Johnson really loves nature, so the family then goes to the Himalayan forest. Solomon and Mary have the time of their lives riding an elephant through the grasslands!

22

At the forest, the trip guide shows the kids many other lovely animals, including the amazing Bengal tiger, which is known for its attractive orange and black stripes.

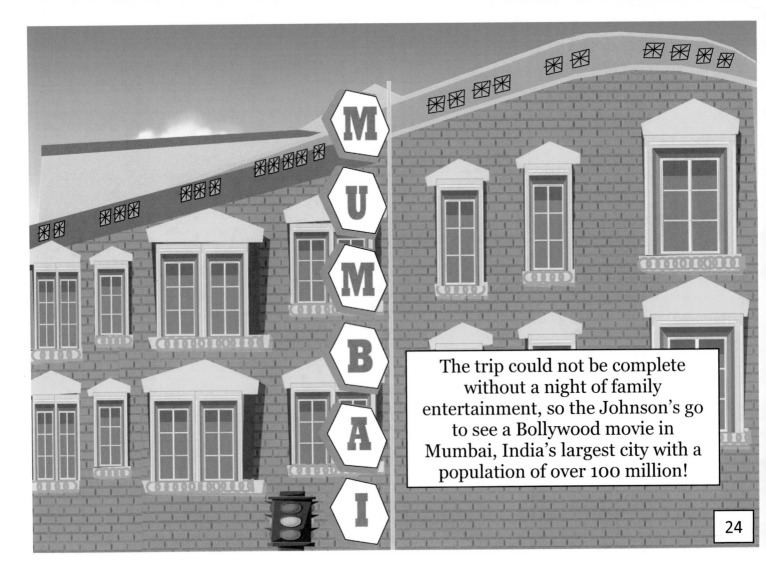

The trip could not be complete without a night of family entertainment, so the Johnson's go to see a Bollywood movie in Mumbai, India's largest city with a population of over 100 million!

It is getting late and time for the Johnson family to return home. They ride a very busy train to the airport in New Delhi, India's capital.

25

Solomon heads back home with new exciting things to share from his great adventure to India!

Made in the USA
Middletown, DE
01 July 2022

68188181R00018